The Three Billy Goats Gruff

Retold by **Bonnie Dobkin**

Illustrated by **Sibi Vohra**

TeachingStrategies™ • Washington D.C.

For Teaching Strategies, Inc.
Publisher: Larry Bram
Editorial Director: Hilary Parrish Nelson
VP Curriculum and Assessment: Cate Heroman
Product Manager: Kai-leé Berke
Book Development Team: Sherrie Rudick and Jan Greenberg
Project Manager: Jo A. Wilson

For Q2AMedia
Editorial Director: Bonnie Dobkin
Editor and Curriculum Adviser: Suzanne Barchers
Program Manager: Gayatri Singh
Creative Director: Simmi Sikka
Project Manager: Santosh Vasudevan
Illustrator: Sibi Vohra
Designer: Neha Kaul

Teaching Strategies, Inc.
P.O. Box 42243
Washington, DC 20015
www.TeachingStrategies.com

ISBN: 978-1-60617-125-7

The Library of Congress has catalogued the Teaching Strategies Big Book edition of this title as:
Dobkin, Bonnie.
  The three billy goats gruff / retold by Bonnie Dobkin ; illustrator, Sibi Vohra.
    p. cm.
  Summary: Three billy goats must outwit the big, ugly troll that lives under the bridge
  they have to cross on their way up the mountain.
  ISBN: 978-1-60617-149-3
  [1. Fairy tales. 2. Folklore—Norway.] I. Vohra, Sibi, ill. II. Asbjørnsen, Peter Christen, 1812–1885.
  Tre bukkene Bruse. English. III. Title.
  PZ8.D650Thr 2010
  398.2—dc22
  [E]
                                              2009037225

CPSIA tracking label information:
RR Donnelley, Shenzhen, China
Date of Production: February 2011
Cohort: Batch 2

Printed and bound in China

  2 3 4 5 6 7 8 9 10   15 14 13 12 11
       Printing   Year Printed

Once upon a time, in a beautiful
green valley, there lived three
brothers who just happened
to be goats. They were
known as the three Billy
Goats Gruff, and they
were as different
as different
could be.

The oldest brother was Big Billy Goat Gruff. He was big, and he was strong, and he was rough, and he was tough. He had thick curvy horns and a head like a boulder, and his hooves crushed the rocks when he walked. He wasn't afraid of anything. (Being big can sometimes make you feel like that.)

The second brother was Middle Billy Goat Gruff. He was half the size of his big brother, and his horns were short and thin. He was a very nervous goat, and he sometimes thought that no one listened to him. (Being in the middle can sometimes make you think like that.)

The youngest brother was Little Billy Goat Gruff. He was a tiny little goat with tiny little hooves, and the nubs of his horns barely poked from the top of his head. He liked to talk, and he thought he was very smart. (Being small can sometimes make you act like that.)

Now, what the three Billy Goats Gruff liked to do more than anything in the world was eat the long green grass in their beautiful valley.

They ate in the morning. They ate in the afternoon. They ate in the evening until the sun went down.

They ate so much that there soon was very little grass left to eat.

"What will we do?" said Middle Billy Goat Gruff. "If we don't find more grass, we'll soon be nothing but skin and bones."

"Then we'll find more grass," said
Big Billy Goat Gruff.

"But where?" asked the middle brother.
"Where are we going to find more grass?"

"I know!" said Little Billy Goat Gruff,
feeling very smart. "We'll go to the
meadow on the other side of the river!
We can stay for days, and eat and eat,
and soon we will be very, very fat!

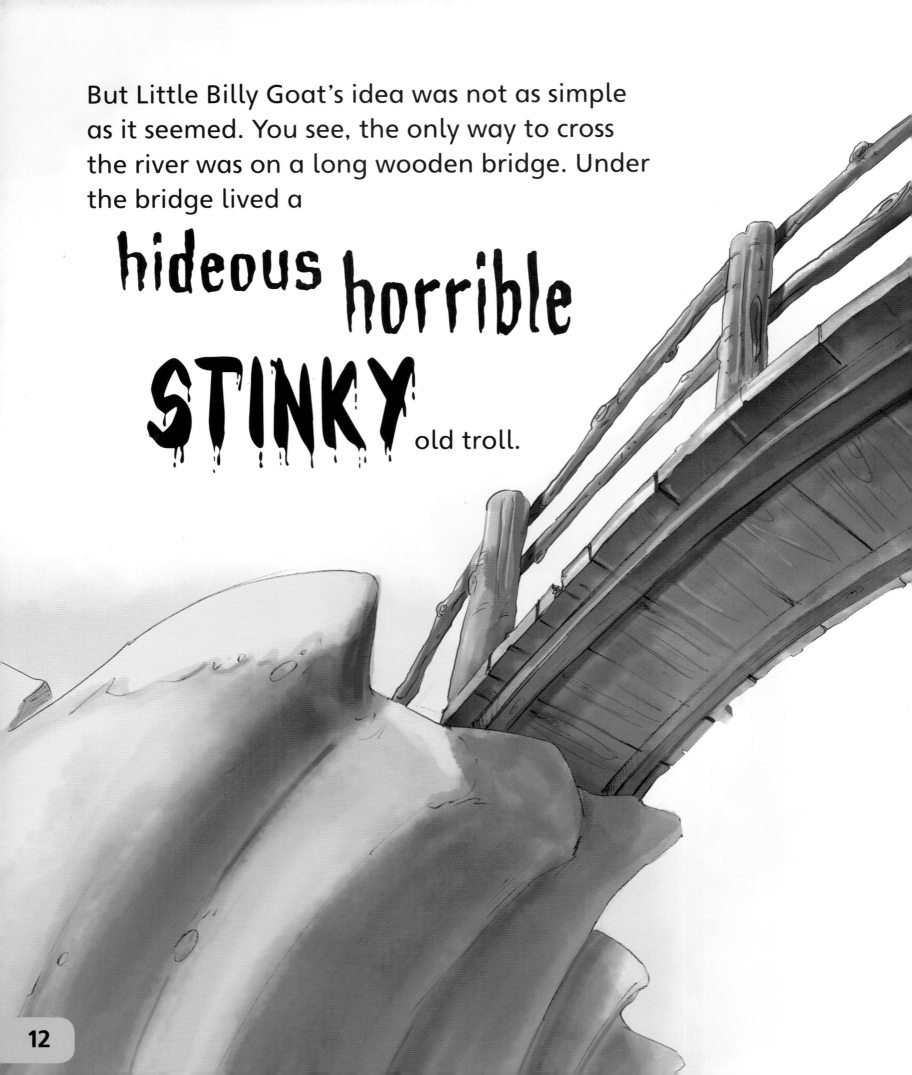

But Little Billy Goat's idea was not as simple as it seemed. You see, the only way to cross the river was on a long wooden bridge. Under the bridge lived a

hideous horrible STINKY old troll.

The troll had bumpy green skin
and great froggy eyes. He had a big
squashed nose that was always dripping.
His teeth were snaggly, his claws were
fraggly, and he smelled like a foot.

Oh, yes.

He also ate anyone who tried to
cross his bridge.

"We can't go across that bridge!" cried Middle Billy Goat Gruff. "What about the troll?"

"I'm not worried about the troll," said Big Billy Goat Gruff.

"Well, I am," said his middle brother. "I don't feel like being eaten for lunch."

"Don't worry," said Little Billy Goat Gruff, feeling very smart indeed. "I have a plan." And he told them what it was.

The next morning,
Little Billy Goat Gruff
set off across the bridge.

Trip-trap, trip-trap,
went his tiny hooves
on the wooden planks.

A terrible roar rose up from below.

"WHO'S TRIP-TRAPPING ACROSS MY BRIDGE?"

"It is only I, Little Billy Goat Gruff,"
said the goat.

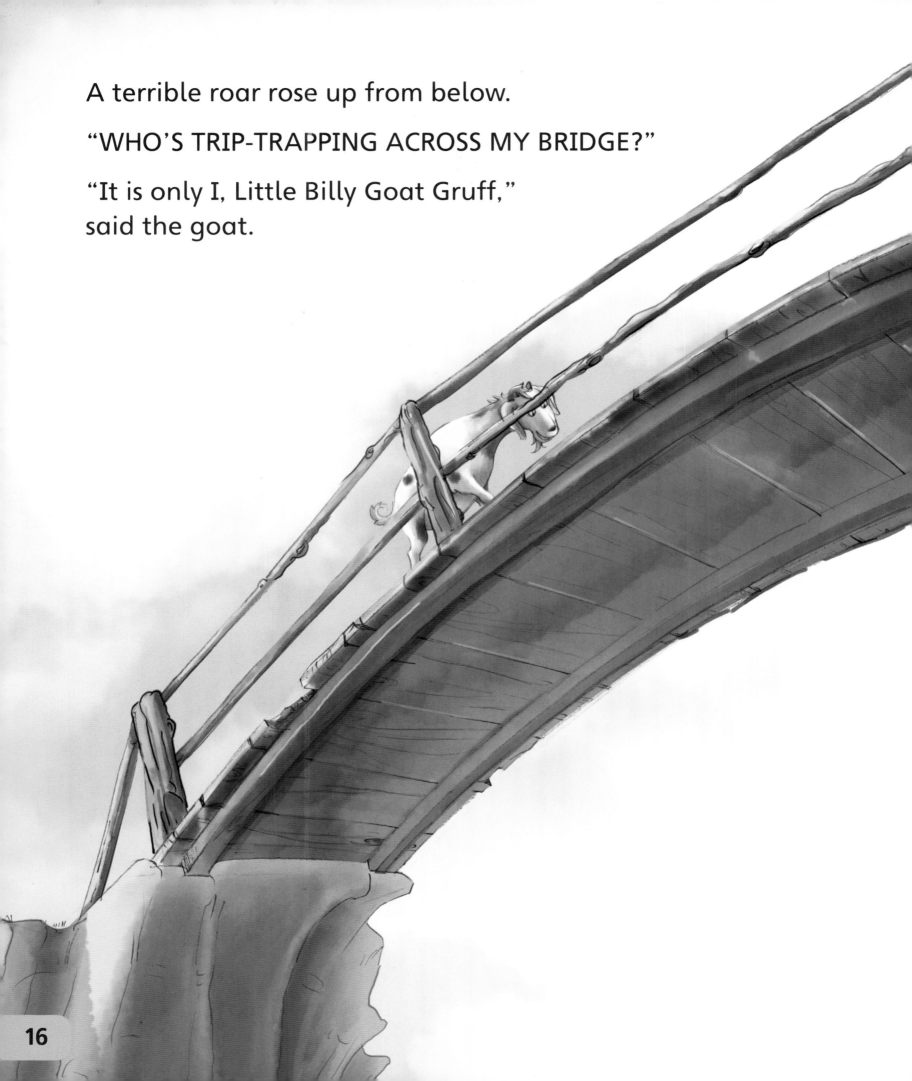

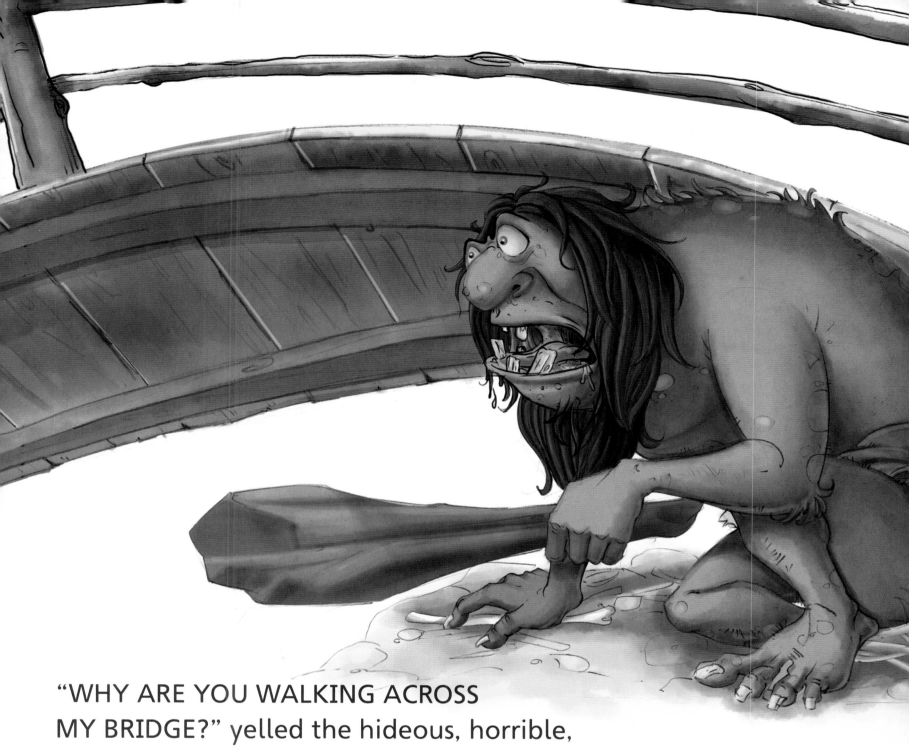

"WHY ARE YOU WALKING ACROSS
MY BRIDGE?" yelled the hideous, horrible,
stinky old troll.

"I'm going to eat the green grass in the meadow
and make myself fat." said the goat.

"OH, NO, YOU'RE NOT!" roared the troll. "BECAUSE
I'M COMING UP TO EAT *YOU*!"

And he leaped on top of the bridge.

Little Billy Goat Gruff trembled where he stood. "Oh, please, Mr. Troll, don't eat me. I'm too small, and you'll be finished in one gulp. Wait for my brother. He's much bigger and fatter than I am."

Hmmm, thought the troll. *Why not? I can always catch you on your way back home.*

"Very well," said the troll, "be off with you."

"Oh, thank you, Mr. Troll," said Little Billy Goat Gruff. And he *trip-trapped* his way to the far side of the bridge and into the meadow.

A little while later, Middle Billy Goat Gruff set off across the bridge.

Clip-clop, clip clop, went his hooves on the wooden planks.

A roar rose up from below.
"WHO'S CLIP-CLOPPING ACROSS MY BRIDGE?"

Middle Billy Goat shook so hard he almost fell down.
"It is only I, M-m-middle Billy Goat Gruff."

"WHY ARE YOU WALKING ACROSS MY BRIDGE?" yelled the hideous, horrible, stinky old troll.

"I'm going to eat the green grass in the meadow and make myself f-f-fat," said the goat.

"OH, NO, YOU'RE NOT!" roared the troll. "BECAUSE I'M COMING UP TO EAT *YOU*!"

And he leaped on top of the bridge.

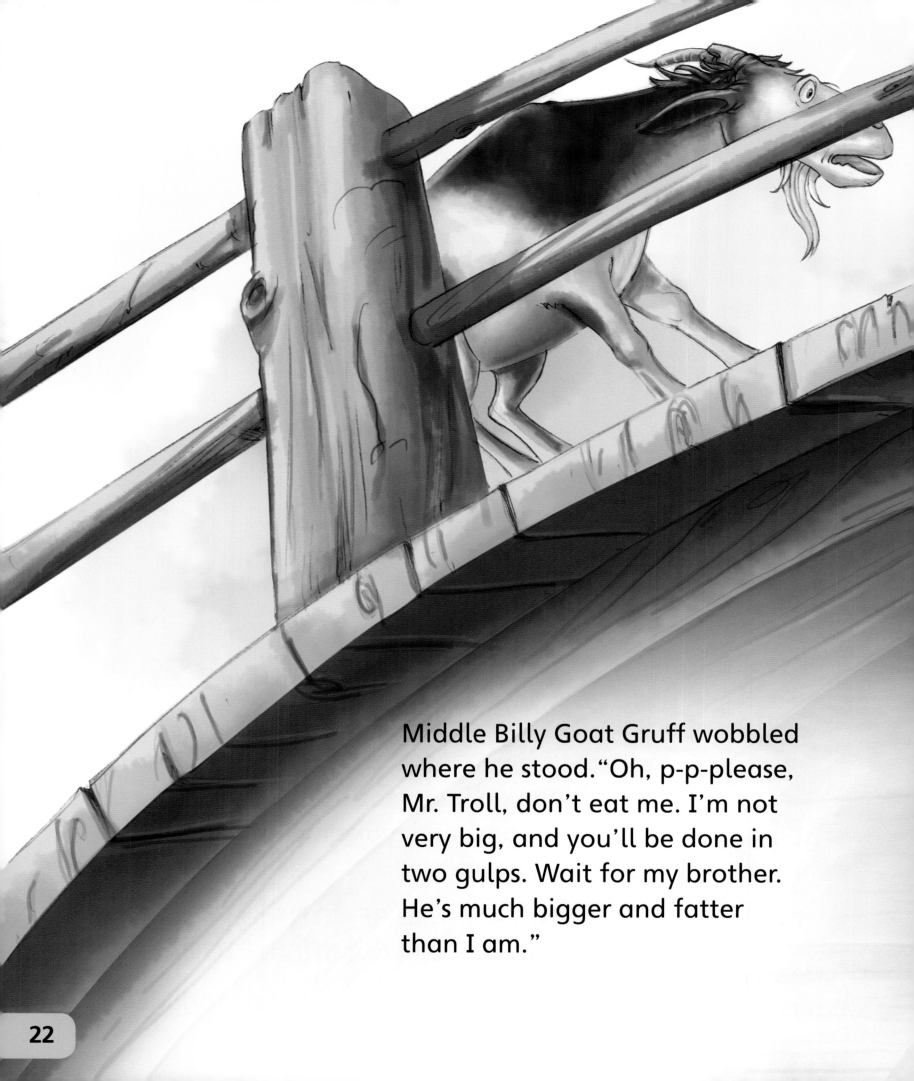

Middle Billy Goat Gruff wobbled where he stood. "Oh, p-p-please, Mr. Troll, don't eat me. I'm not very big, and you'll be done in two gulps. Wait for my brother. He's much bigger and fatter than I am."

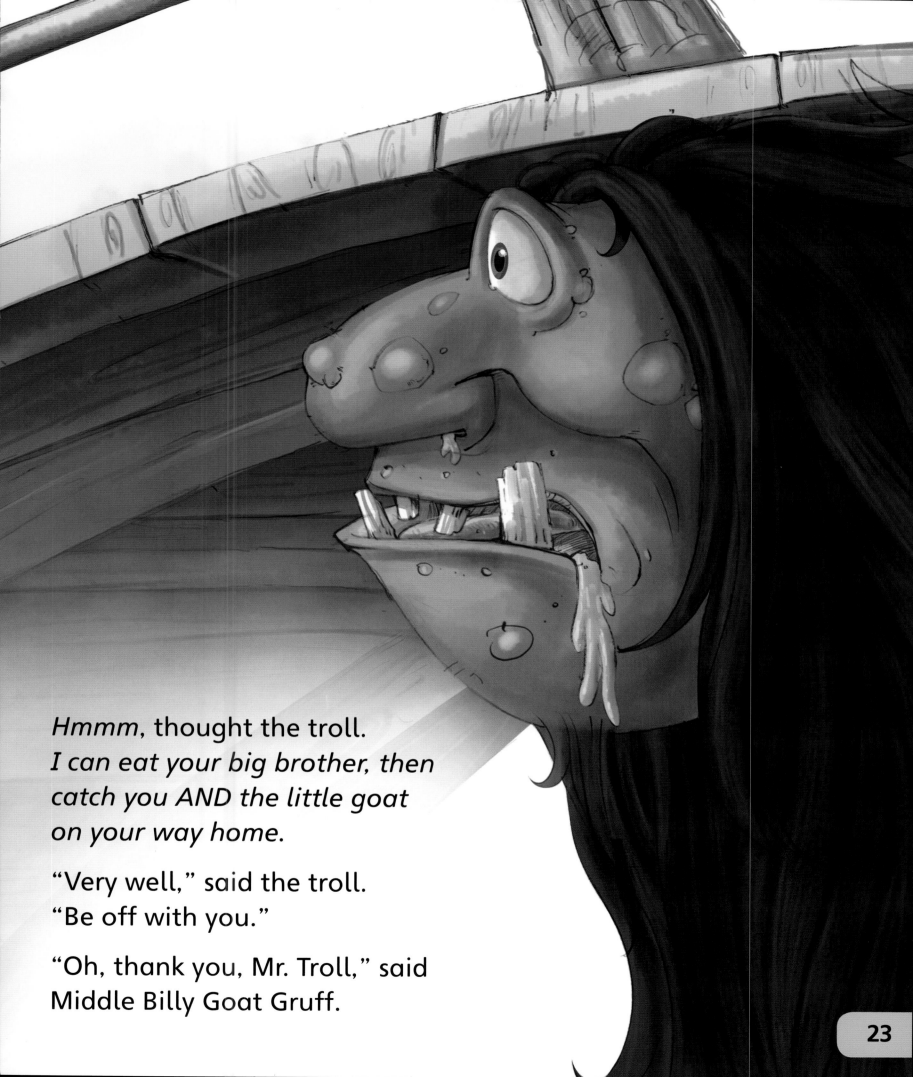

Hmmm, thought the troll.
*I can eat your big brother, then
catch you AND the little goat
on your way home.*

"Very well," said the troll.
"Be off with you."

"Oh, thank you, Mr. Troll," said
Middle Billy Goat Gruff.

23

And he *clip-clopped* as fast as his hooves could take him to the far side of the bridge and into the meadow.

A little while later, when the sun was high in the sky, Big Billy Goat Gruff set off across the bridge.

TROMP. TROMP. TROMP. TROMP
went his hooves on the wooden planks.

A roar rose up from below.

"WHO'S TROMP-TROMPING
ACROSS MY BRIDGE?"

"It is I, Big Billy
Goat Gruff," said
the goat.

"WHY ARE YOU WALKING ACROSS MY BRIDGE?" yelled the hideous, horrible, stinky old troll.

"I'm going to eat the green grass in the meadow and make myself fat."

"OH, NO, YOU'RE NOT!" roared the troll. "BECAUSE I'M COMING UP TO EAT *YOU*!"

"Well," said Big Billy Goat Gruff. "What are you waiting for?"

And the troll leaped on top of the bridge.

Big Billy Goat Gruff stared at the troll.

The troll stared at Big Billy Goat Gruff.

Then Big Billy Goat lowered his head and charged!

He knocked the troll down with his big hard head.

He stomped on the troll with his huge, sharp hooves.

Then he picked the troll up with his long curved horns and tossed him high into the air!

The troll spun in circles and dropped into the river with a great splash! As the rushing waters carried him away, he shouted and spouted and spit and screamed—and yelled something nasty about goats.

That was the last anyone ever saw of the hideous, horrible, stinky old troll.

And the three Billy Goats Gruff? They lived happily in the valley for the rest of their lives, eating the green, green grass on both sides of the river. And getting very fat.